OHIO DOMINICAN COLLEGE 1911

LIBRARY

1216 SUNBURY RD.
COLUMBUS, OHIO

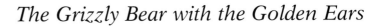

The Grizzly Bear with the Golden Ears

The Grizzly Bear with the Golden Ears

by Jean Craighead George
Pictures by Tom Catania

Harper & Row, Publishers

The people of the North called her Golden Ears.
She had round blond ears that set
her apart from all other bears.
She was a brown grizzly bear of Alaska,
the great bear the Eskimos worshipped
because it walks like a man.

Golden Ears lived in the ice-bitten forest of Katmai.
In the summer she and the other bears of the forest
fished for salmon in the Brooks River. In autumn they
wandered the mountains eating blueberries and cranberries,
and in the winter when ice storms crackled, they slept under
the roots of the spruce trees in the foothills of the rugged
Aleutian Mountains.

4

5

Golden Ears was three years old.

One sunny noon in June
she brought her little golden-eared cub
to meet the bears of the Brooks River,
who were gathered on the riverbank.

The bears stepped back and lowered their heads,
for a mother bear with a cub is both queen and king,
the most adored bear of all bears.
Even Ursus stepped back. He was the one-thousand-pound male
grizzly who had killed a little cub, as some male bears do
when they find one alone and unguarded.

Below Brooks Falls the red salmon
gathered by the thousands to leap
up the waterfall.
The fish leave the Pacific Ocean and swim up the rivers
to the same streamlets where they were born.

There in the shallows under the starflowers and blue gentians,
they lay their eggs and die.
As they swim home they are eaten by wolves, eagles, gulls
and, along the Brooks River, by the people at fish camp,
the ranger and the rollicking, diving, wonderful
brown grizzly bears.

Golden Ears splashed into the churning water.
She snapped at a fish and missed.
Golden Ears swatted another fish
and missed.

In a pool nearby, Kasvik, her friend,
put her head under the water,
saw a salmon, snapped her jaws and caught it.
She carried it up on the shore.
Golden Ears wanted that fish. She was boss bear, so
she lunged at Kasvik, bluffing her, as bears do.
Kasvik dropped the salmon and ran. Golden Ears
sat down by her golden-eared cub, cleaned the bones from
the fish and daintily ate it.

The next day she bluffed Kuka and took his fish.
And the following day
she pounced at her sister and took her fish.
Feeling very sure of herself, she walked up to Ursus.
"Yarl," she growled.
The enormous grizzly dropped his fish
and backed away.

Golden Ears did not bother to fish,
she just bluffed all
the bears on the Brooks River and
ate until she was full.

Then she romped with her cub
in the aspen grove
and watched the eaglets
in their nest.

One summer afternoon when the sun flashed on the river,
Golden Ears came upon a fisherman who was pulling
a huge fish out of a pool.

She hesitated, because she was afraid of people;
but she was boss bear.
She charged the fisherman.
He dropped rod, reel, bait and lunch,
and ran in terror back to fish camp to
report the terrible bear with the golden ears.

Out in the river, Golden Ears tore open the lunch bag
and found chocolate bars, ham sandwiches and cake.
She carried them back to the aspen grove, and she
and her cub devoured them.

Ursus stalked the forest behind them.

When the winds of August blew and the eaglets took their
first flight over the Brooks River, the salmon run slowed down.
The bears of the Brooks River caught fewer and fewer fish.
A young boy came to the waterfall and cast his line,
caught a big salmon and hauled it ashore.

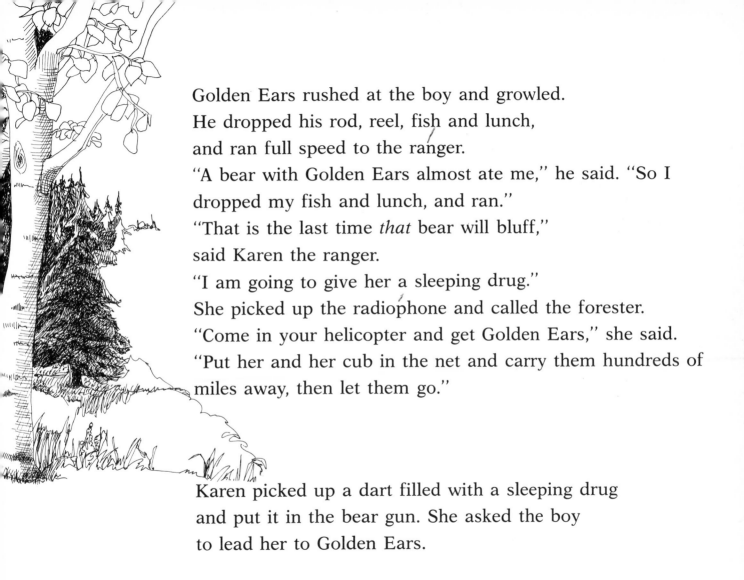

Golden Ears rushed at the boy and growled.
He dropped his rod, reel, fish and lunch,
and ran full speed to the ranger.
"A bear with Golden Ears almost ate me," he said. "So I
dropped my fish and lunch, and ran."
"That is the last time *that* bear will bluff,"
said Karen the ranger.
"I am going to give her a sleeping drug."
She picked up the radiophone and called the forester.
"Come in your helicopter and get Golden Ears," she said.
"Put her and her cub in the net and carry them hundreds of
miles away, then let them go."

Karen picked up a dart filled with a sleeping drug
and put it in the bear gun. She asked the boy
to lead her to Golden Ears.

Golden Ears was eating sandwiches and chocolate in the aspen grove.
Ursus was nearby. Presently he lumbered past them and
dove into the river. He belly flopped on a salmon, and
Golden Ears got to her feet.
She challenged Ursus. He ran up the bank, and the fish was hers.
When she had cleaned and eaten the fish she climbed back to her cub.

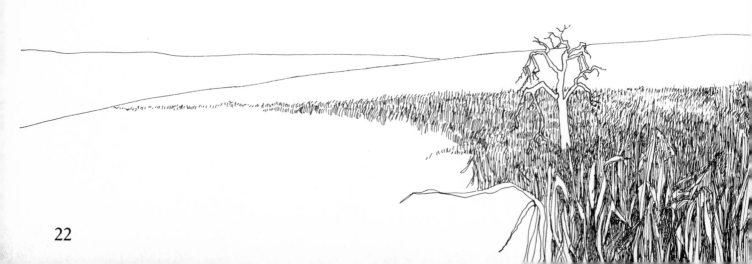

He was gone.

The odor of the male grizzly Ursus mingled with the scent of her little cub.
She looked for him in the aspen grove.
She searched the meadow, ran through the flowers.
She called and roared in anguish.

She thundered into the forest out of sight of the ranger,
knocking down trees, uprooting ferns and moss as she hunted for her cub.
Then she stood up,
and walking on two feet, she sniffed and called.
No little cub answered.

All night Golden Ears searched the riverbank.
She woofed and cried and suffered.
Just before the misty morning dawned,
she lowered her head;
and the once proud Golden Ears
shuffled miserably
toward her den on the mountain.

The bears of the Brooks River stood still and listened.
"Woof," Golden Ears called (Where are you, little one?).
"Woof."
"Woof."
A gray wolf howled, the eaglets called and
Golden Ears gave up the hunt. She walked in silence.

"Wuf," came a small voice.

A tree swayed. Golden Ears snapped up her head, rose to her hind feet and stared.

In the top of the spruce her golden-eared cub looked down at her.

Golden Ears whimpered and woofed
as her cub backed into her arms.
She flopped back on her haunches and hugged him.
She licked, kissed and loved him.

Then she got to her feet.
Her cub close to her heels, she tramped down the mountain,
crossed the Brooks River, and
jogged along the shore of Lake Naknek,
around the rocky foot of Mount Katolinat
and out across the marshland.

She passed a moose, walked under clouds of swallows,
and trotted for miles and miles to the shores of the Margot River.

On the riverbank she twitched her golden ears
and watched hordes of salmon swim by.
Then, with a loud ker-splash, she dove,
came up with a fish
and never went back to the bears of the Brooks River.

To

ESTHER STEVENS CRAIGHEAD

with love

The Grizzly Bear with the Golden Ears
Text copyright © 1982 by Jean Craighead George
Illustrations copyright © 1982 by Tom C. Catania
For information address
Harper & Row, Publishers, Inc., 10 East 53rd Street,
New York, N.Y. 10022. Published simultaneously in
Canada by Fitzhenry & Whiteside Limited, Toronto.

Library of Congress Cataloging in Publication Data
George, Jean Craighead, date
　The grizzly bear with the golden ears.

　Summary: A grizzly bear who bluffs rather than
hunts for her food learns an important lesson.
　　1. Grizzly bear—Legends and stories.　[1. Grizzly
bear—Fiction.　2. Bears—Fiction]　I. Catania,
Tom.　II. Title
PZ10.3.G316Gr 1982　　　[E]　　　80-7908
ISBN 0-06-021965-3　　　　　　AACR2
ISBN 0-06-021966-1 (lib. bdg.)

First Edition